A ROOKIE READER®

MESSY BESSEY'S GARDEN

By Patricia and Fredrick McKissack

Illustrated by Richard Hackney

Prepared under the direction of Robert Hillerich, Ph.D.

CHILDRENS PRESS®
CHICAGO

Library of Congress Cataloging-in-Publication Data

McKissack, Pat, 1944-
    Messy Bessey's garden / by Patricia and Fredrick
McKissack ; illustrated by Richard Hackney.
      p. cm. — (A Rookie reader)
    Summary: Messy Bessey discovers that with proper
care her garden will flourish.
    ISBN 0-516-02008-0
    [1. Gardening—Fiction. 2. Stories in rhyme.]
I. McKissack, Fredrick. II. Hackney, Richard, ill.
III. Title. IV. Series.
PZ8.3.M4598Mf   1991
[E]—dc20
                         91-15333
                            CIP
                            AC

It's Spring again, Miss Bessey.
No more ice and snow.

3

j42822

Come. It's time to plant your seeds.
And watch your garden grow.

5

Dig a hole.

Put in a seed.

Plant them row by row.

Cover them up.
Water them well.

10

11

Now, let the garden grow.

14

No, no, no, Messy Bessey!
Plants need help to grow.

16

You haven't taken care of them.
You've let your garden go.

18

So get the shovel.
Get the hoe.

Water every row.

Pull the weeds.

Snip and cut.

Help your garden grow.

Fall has come at last, Miss Bess.

Now, don't you feel just fine?
Your garden is a big success—

with pumpkins on the vine!

WORD LIST

a	fine	Miss	so
again	garden	more	Spring
and	get	messy	success
at	go	need	taken
Bess	grow	no	the
Bessey	has	now	them
big	haven't	of	time
by	help	on	to
care	hoe	plant	vine
come	hole	pull	up
cover	ice	pumpkins	watch
cut	in	put	water
dig	is	row	weeds
don't	it's	seed	well
every	just	shovel	with
Fall	last	snip	you
feel	let	snow	your
			you've

About the Authors

Patricia and **Fredrick McKissack** are free-lance writers, editors, and owners of All-Writing Services, a family business located in Clayton, Missouri. They are award-winning authors whose titles have been honored with the Coretta Scott King Award, the Jane Addams Peace Award, and the Parent's Choice Award. Pat's book *Mirandy and Brother Wind*, illustrated by Jerry Pinkney, was a 1989 Caldecott Honor Book.

The McKissacks have authored over twenty books for Childrens Press, including biographies in the People of Distinction series, *The Start-Off Stories*, *The Civil Rights Movement in America from 1865 to Present*, and seven Rookie Readers, including three Messy Bessey adventures.

In addition to writing, the McKissacks are often speakers at educational meetings, workshops, and seminars. They have three grown sons; the oldest, Fredrick, Jr., is a sportswriter. When they aren't working on books, the McKissacks enjoy working in their garden. That's where the idea for this book originated. "A successful garden takes a lot of work," says Fred.

About the Artist

Richard Hackney is a San Francisco illustrator and writer who graduated from Art Center School in Los Angeles, California. He has worked at Disney Studios, drawn a syndicated comic strip, and has been an art director in advertising. He has also done some acting, written children's stories, and currently is doing a lot of educational illustration.

Richard lives with his wife, Elizabeth, and a black cat in a home on the edge of San Francisco Bay.